"Store's all out of bread. It's not raining or snowing and the weather is fine, otherwise I'd go out and grab a movie or dine..."

For Every Family

March 21, 2020

Text © 2021 by Meaghan Racicot

Illustration © 2021 by Marybeth Lensel

All rights reserved. Published by Meaghan Racicot

www.MeaghanRacicot.com

Text, images, and associated logos are trademarks and/or registered trademarks of Meaghan Racicot.

No part of this publication may be reproduced without proper notation of publisher, author, and illustrator.

Stuck Inside

by Meaghan Racicot

I can't do too much, and it's not just me.

The whole family is here.
How can this be?

All the laundry is done. And so are the chores.

All the games

are all played.

All the cakes

have been made.

"Ready or not! Here.... I... COME!!!!!"

All the shows have been seen.

And the dishes are clean.

I'm stuck in the house. The whole family is here...

"Meow!"

until this time next year!!!

Meaghan Racicot is a mom of two and full time poet/author whose other books include "Tomatoes!" and "The Sky Ahead".

She lives with her family in Auburn, Massachusetts, and loves reading, writing, and rock n' roll!

Check out her imagination on Instagram and at www.MeaghanRacicot.com.

CPSIA information can be obtained
at www.ICGtesting.com
Printed in the USA
BVHW021118200621
609986BV00002B/3